Strait Jackets And Rubber Chickens

Recovering from Trauma and Mental Health Difficulties

Christina Davies

Case I.D: 1-15133626061

This book is based on the author's personal experiences with trauma, depression, and borderline personality disorder. It is not intended to provide medical, psychological, or professional advice, nor should it be used as a substitute for diagnosis or treatment. Readers are encouraged to seek appropriate professional support where needed.

The names and identifying details of individuals have been changed to protect anonymity, unless otherwise stated in direct quotations for reference purposes.

978-1-972710-26-5

First Edition, 2026

The purpose of this book is not to give a definition of depression nor personality disorder and is not in any way meant to be used as a textbook, but rather it is the memoir of how I experienced depression and borderline personality disorder and how various people helped me survive and overcome the trauma of rape. The names given in the book are pseudonyms to maintain anonymity, unless there has been a direct quote where the true name is given as a point of reference.

Table of Contents

Prologue 1

Chapter 1 How Deep Is Your Love 4

Chapter 2 Hear Me Roar 9

Chapter 3 Better When I'm Dancing 21

Chapter 4 Learn to Be Human Too 34

Chapter 5 Demons 49

Chapter 6 Save Me 61

Chapter 7 Man in the Mirror 69

Chapter 8 This Woman's Work 76

Chapter 9 Bring me to Life 85

Epilogue 89

PROLOGUE

October 1992

I was excited. My best friend Claire and I had been talking about the dinner and dance, held by the local Young Farmers club, all week. I didn't have a boyfriend, but Claire did, and we spent time in class talking about who was going and who I might be partnered up with during the dinner. The evening came and Claire and I had a lovely time. Claire and her boyfriend sat on one side of the table, and I found myself sitting next to a friend's friend on the other. He was chatty during the meal and gave me a lot of attention. I wore an emerald-green ball dress that had once belonged to my sister. I felt like a princess.

After the dinner and dance, both Claire and I went to stay at Claire's boyfriend's home. He had a small, two-bedroom house and a lot of friends were there, including the guy I had sat with at dinner. Before I knew it, we found ourselves sitting next to each other again as we watched television, and after a couple of drinks we began snogging and ended up in the bathroom together. The house was small and there was nowhere else that was private. I had had a boyfriend before, and although young, innocent, and somewhat naïve, I was aware of the boundaries to intimacy. However, he was persistent and although I had on more than one occasion during the encounter said that I didn't want sex, as I wanted to keep my chastity until marriage, one thing led to another. It wasn't until he was on top of me and exerting his male dominance upon me that I realised that 'halfway doesn't count' actually does count! I was being *raped.* I wondered whether I should try and fight him off, or call for help, but I had had some alcohol, and I didn't think that anyone would hear me or that I would be strong enough to push him off. Paralysed with fear, all I could do was to wait for him to finish and the tumult would be over. Little did I realise what the consequences of that event would have upon me in future years.

The following morning, I woke up bleeding, and it was then a dawning realisation of what had happened came upon me. Apart from waiting for my period to start, I blocked the event out of my mind and carried on as normal for following days, weeks and years.

I went to university, met the man of my dreams, and had a whirlwind romance, leading to marriage just eighteen months later. It was not until my son, then aged five, was involved in a safeguarding incident at school, that the memories and injustice of the rape came to the fore and subsequently shattered my world for the following eight years. Depression set in and I was also diagnosed as having borderline personality disorder (BPD).

CHAPTER 1

How Deep Is Your Love

Your eyes see me now.
The morning sun shines brightly.
I feel depths of love.

So, a bit about me, to give a little background to my core beliefs and how I've got to be where I'm at now.

The earliest memory I can recall was a snowy winter's day in December 1977. I was two years and 11 months old. My family (Mum, Dad, and older sister by ten years) were moving house. A close family friend was looking after my sister and I whilst Mum and Dad did the hard work of moving. The snow had settled and was thick on the ground.

Our friend's mother (my aunty, as we called close family friends 'aunt' and 'uncle' back then) was able to find snow boots for my sister, but my feet were too small to borrow a pair, and that is my first memory of feeling jealous and left out. My sister and my auntie's children were older than me and I felt so left out as I was so much younger and wanted to be 'grown up' just like them.

We made our way to the new house and Mum washed me in the sink in her bedroom, as it was late and I guess she was too tired from the stress of the day to give me a full bath.

I had a happy childhood, and I was very close to my mother as I was raised almost as an only child. My sister was like an extra mother to me, being ten years older than myself. The age gap was so big as my parents had lost a child in infancy due to multiple medical conditions. My brother's picture was on the windowsill, and I was acutely aware that he had been a part of my parents and sister's lives, but that I would never know him. He was five years old when he departed from this life, and I was born just 11 months later. As a child I would occasionally find my mum crying and understood that she was feeling sad because of the loss of her dear son. This grief process was the beginning of my deep-rooted core belief that "I must be good". I didn't want to be naughty or upset my mum and make her cry. My father never talked about my brother and I knew better than to ask my father about him.

My father was an extremely hard-working man and commuted into London every day as a surveyor for a large Chartered Surveyors company. I cherished my time with him at the weekends and loved climbing onto his lap and he would sing songs to me and tell me stories about his childhood and how mischievous he was!

My sister was my idol and someone I aspired to be like. She always seemed so grown up and together with my mum, I lapped up the love and attention they gave me. I was seven when my sister left home to commence nursing training. The day her acceptance letter came in the post she was working down the road from where we lived in the local newsagents. My parents made me run and take the letter to her – I was still in my pyjamas! I felt so embarrassed but gave her the letter, excited because Mum and Dad were excited, however I didn't comprehend what it meant for me. I cried for days when my sister left home and missed her so terribly! With my childlike understanding, I thought she had wanted to leave me and couldn't understand that it was just part of her own journey to independence.

Life was quiet for a while, and my parents bought me a puppy dog who I lavished love on. I looked forward to coming home from school every day to see my puppy and give her lots of cuddles and play games with her. Then, one summer's day, an awful accident occurred, and my puppy was killed. It was my fault, although no one EVER blamed me for the accident. I was distraught and that was my second real experience of grief – the first being my sister leaving home. I felt so ashamed of myself and became quite introverted and quiet for a long time. I wouldn't let anyone talk about my puppy and glared at them if they dared to mention her name! That time of my life then became difficult for us as a family. My grandparents lost their home due to financial stressors, my mum's sister was diagnosed with Multiple Sclerosis, and my grandfather was diagnosed with Parkinson's disease.

My family follow the Christian faith and church life played a big part in my childhood. I was an active member of our local church, going to the youth groups, and singing in the choir. In my teenage years my mother did pastoral counselling training, and upon early retirement my father was ordained as a vicar. The values that this lifestyle instilled in me were to be good, proper, respectful and to be contained in demonstrating emotions.

CHAPTER 2

Hear Me Roar

Unleash the tiger!
Roar! Thunders in the battle
The tiger is free.

I found myself to be a capable woman, living a very happy life with my husband and three children. After university I worked in manufacturing for several years and then decided to train as a registered nurse. I managed to juggle my career with family life and felt fulfilled in all I did. My career progressed and I developed my zeal for nursing into a passion for supporting young children and their families and entered training for Health Visiting. I felt complete and totally fulfilled in life until September 2013, when my world and all reality crumbled around me. My son was victim to some vulgar behaviour from another child at school. This behaviour triggered memories of being raped and it was the first time that I felt so unsafe and suicidal that my husband wouldn't even leave me to have a bath on my own.

At first, my attention was on supporting my son and working through how he could be kept safe at school. Naturally, a safeguarding concern was raised with the multi-agency safeguarding hub by the school and I was furious with this. I was doing my safeguarding module as part of my Health Visitor training and was concerned that my training would be in jeopardy. I raised a complaint with the school governors; however, the complaint wasn't upheld. My relationship with the school became tarnished as I had been the Chair of Governors just a few years previously. I hated doing the school run as I didn't want to see the mother of the child that had behaved inappropriately towards my son, and I was worried that other parents might know what had happened. The Trust and university that I was studying with were, however, very supportive and gave me time to process what had happened and even offered for me to take a break from the course and rejoin at a later date. I was determined to complete the course and managed to do so, coming out with a fantastic grade at the end, however it had come at a personal cost. I immersed myself in work and tried to ignore the fact that I had been raped. However, there were many mornings I went into work and just cried. I was tired of dealing with the trauma and the memories of the rape were very much at the forefront of my mind.

Depression set in and life changed. There are many definitions for depression but for me, I think it is a debilitating illness that has a profound effect on the person suffering from it and on those around them. At my worst, my husband would describe me as looking like a zombie, with the life sucked out of me. I became withdrawn and detached, and although I was present in body, my head and mind were numb and unable to process the reality of what had happened. I found it a struggle to engage with my loved ones, to the point that I felt I would rather be dead than never be able to feel love, affection and kindness in the way that I once had.

I found depression to be exhausting and it started to take a lot of effort to get up and dressed in the morning. Socialising and seeing friends took a lot out of me and I found that I needed time to recover after any purposeful interaction with others. I reflected that this is why people with depression may opt out of social events – it is not a reflection of others or deliberate, it is just that the effort of getting ready, travelling to the event, and socialising is just too overwhelming and exhausting. At my worst, my mind and speech slowed down, as did my walking. I felt as though I was a car running on empty!

I became very tearful, and during one particular evening I found myself having very strong urges to self-harm. These urges were initially pacified with scratches, but over the next few years I progressed to cutting, burning, and ligaturing myself, along with smoking cigarettes, as methods of self-harming. I had temporary relief from my feelings with these methods, however I found that they did not bring long-term comfort. My feelings of self-destruction, guilt and pain were so intense that I felt I needed to be punished for the rape and what had happened to my son. I did not feel worthy of being kind to myself.

The depression took its toll on me, and in 2018 I felt so suicidal that I took an overdose. This was then repeated on subsequent occasions. The effect on my family was devastating. The schools that my children were in were very supportive of them and offered counselling and time out of class if a challenging subject was being discussed. My daughters became very protective of me, and my son needed a lot of reassurance that I was ok and that I still loved him.

I found that keeping a journal was therapeutic, and one day I wrote my 'goodbye letters'. It was never my intention to end my life, however when my joy and sense of hope was gone, I yearned to be no more. My sister was on the end of the phone on several occasions listening to me say that I did not care whether I lived or died.

You may ask what about my family? Did I not want to stay alive for them? On good days my answer was, of course I did! I looked to the small, everyday things that I loved and cherished, i.e., holding my son's hand when out for a walk, kissing my children goodnight, cooking a nice meal for my family, a tender kiss from my husband. On a bad day, however, these small things lost significance and I felt numb to the love that my family had for me.

The thing with depression is that you lose interest in all the things you once held dear. I used to love baking, cooking and shopping for the ingredients to cook a nice meal. Over the years, my husband began to do the shopping and eventually I re-joined him. Even today, we go shopping together as I would find it too overwhelming to do a big family shop on my own. Housework became a thing of the past and it was not until 2020 that I started to take an interest in my home again and took pride in my identity as a homemaker.

The first meal I cooked from scratch was for my daughter's 18th birthday celebration meal, when we had my parents over for lunch. This was the first meal I had cooked for a good couple of years! I felt very pleased with myself, and this was one of the first glimpses of my recovery. It may not seem like much to be able to cook a meal from scratch but the organisation, vegetable prep and having the actual energy and motivation to do something productive is a lot when you have depression. I cooked the meal, and my husband served it as I didn't have the confidence to portion the meal out appropriately. The meal was a success, and I was pleased with myself for doing something nice for the family.

I finally learnt to live with the depression and learnt when I was starting to dip. Medication helped and I started to see the joy in life again, however the 'black dog' was always there in the background ready to loom large if I didn't take control of it or listen to the cues that it needed taming again. I learnt the things I needed to do each day to keep myself well and these included things such as going for a walk, doing some crafting (I love knitting), speaking/engaging with family and doing some form of mindfulness or meditation. My sleep patterns are generally good, although when I start waking in the night this is usually the first sign that I need to take stock of what is going on and to look after myself more. I am lucky in that I don't have nightmares about the rape, as I know some survivors do. I have many flashbacks, though, and these can lead me to feeling unsafe, thus the spirals of pain and hurt start again and my urges to self-harm become stronger.

I've now explained about my experience with depression, but I haven't explained my battle with borderline personality disorder yet. This is a whole different kettle of fish! It's a condition that affects emotions and how one thinks and feels and responds to situations and relationships. It is characterised by nine factors, those being 1) the fear of abandonment; 2) intense and unstable relationships; 3) a distorted sense of self; 4) impulsive behaviour; 5) self-harming behaviour and recurring thoughts of suicide; 6) intense and highly changeable moods; 7) chronic feelings of emptiness; 8) intense anger and 9) feelings of dissociation. I was diagnosed with BPD during one of my admissions to hospital in 2019, and it took me a long time to accept the diagnosis. The main characteristics I identify with are having a distorted sense of self, self-harming behaviour and recurring thoughts of suicide, intense mood swings, chronic feelings of emptiness, intense anger, and feelings of dissociation. So, all fun – not!

The distorted sense of self comes from having a low self-esteem, and I feel inadequate compared to everyone else I meet. I feel disgusting and shameful because of the rape. Self-harming is a complex matter. I call it 'destructive coping' because that's what it is. Self-harm only hurts oneself and leaves scars. The first time I self-harmed was shortly after the safeguarding incident with my son, and I was sitting at my computer writing an essay for my Health Visiting degree. At first, I started with scratching myself with my fingers and this felt liberating at the time, but then I progressed onto more severe methods. My aim with self-harm was to punish myself. No one else, just myself.

There are lots of self-help guides which give advice on how not to self-harm and what to do instead when the urges arrive, however I still struggled to grapple with the sense of relief I felt when I self-harmed, because I felt like I was letting out my pain, anger and frustration.

I am ashamed of my self-harming, and I kept it a secret from my parents for a long time. Indeed, I have tried to keep the cuts and scratches to a minimum to protect my children, and so I have utilised other methods such as smoking and overeating as a form of punishment. Whilst I was in hospital, I discovered that ligaturing was an effective form of self-harm as the tightness around my neck brought me great relief from the anger and hatred I harboured towards myself. Although I understood the risks of ligaturing and that I could end my life through it, it became a way of expressing the pain I held within myself.

Over time, I have learnt to utilise other methods of expressing my pain and anger other than harming myself. When the urges arrive, I 'ride the wave' and use distraction techniques to help. These include having a bath, sitting watching TV, doing a wordsearch or knitting. I avoid being in the kitchen due to the sharp knives and often use my 'comfort box' to help with distracting myself. My comfort box is a small box that contains items that appeal to my senses. For example, it contains nice memories and pictures that my children have drawn for me, and it has some nice, scented hand cream, and a small piece of sea glass for me to hold in my hand and appreciate its smoothness.

Referring back to the characteristics of BPD, I do have intense moods and feel things very strongly. This doesn't mean to say I'm moody and irritable all the time, because I'm not. The chronic feelings of emptiness are horrible; nothing can fill the void. I feel so ungrateful when I feel empty as I am blessed with so much – a loving family, great friends and a beautiful home. I have a career I can return to if I want, however the void sucks all that up and leaves me feeling stripped of everything. It is partly due to this emptiness that my urges to overdose surface. I want to hibernate and wake up feeling fulfilled and in a better place psychologically. The anger is something that I have battled with. Up until recently, if I allowed myself to feel angry then this would have led to urges to self-harm; but now I am learning to sit with the emotion of anger and let it be and unfold. Dissociation is an odd thing to describe. I would describe it as being present in body but not in mind. I stop engaging with what is going on in the here and now, and phase myself out as a form of self-protection.

There are many reasons why people develop BPD and one of them is teenage sexual trauma – hmmmm, I wonder where I got that from! Please excuse the sarcasm, but to be given a diagnosis of a personality disorder kind of sucks. Though the good thing is that the appropriate support was then put in place to help me manage my thoughts and emotions and it acknowledged the intense feelings of emptiness and dissociation that I had been feeling.

CHAPTER 3

Better When I'm Dancing

Reverberating!
I have dance, I have rhythm.
Joined, we are better.

Is it ever anyone's intention to be hospitalised in a psychiatric unit on at least 13 different occasions? Well, it certainly wasn't mine, but this became part of my reality over an eight-year period.

The first time I was admitted was on the second year anniversary of what my son had been involved in at school. My mindset had been stable until my parents went away and they asked me to water their plants. Whilst I was at their home, I had an overwhelming urge to do damage to their beautiful, grey, leather sofa. It was not because I wanted to hurt or harm my parents in any way whatsoever, but that the sofa represented perfection and my head and heart were starting to feel a long way from being 'perfect'. I went home and told my husband how I felt, and he said that I needed help. I can't remember the process of getting help at that time except that a psychiatrist from the Crisis Team came out to see me at home and immediately admitted me to hospital. On this occasion I only stayed the weekend. I was admitted to the short-stay ward and the only thing I remember about that particular stay was having a meeting with two male psychiatrists and one male nurse. I felt so intimidated as I was the only female talking to men about rape and the safeguarding event with my son. The conclusion from the meeting was that I could be discharged with the premise that I get some in-depth counselling to address the issues stemming from the rape.

Since this first incident, I have had recurrent episodes of feeling suicidal and it was decided that the best way for me to stay safe was to be in hospital. These subsequent stays ranged from one to ten weeks in duration!

I had never been a patient in hospital before, except to have my children, and it was a bizarre feeling. With my nursing background I felt like I should be the professional, ensuring that everyone was alright. I should have been the one in the nurses' office writing notes and discussing cases. It took several admissions for me to accept that I was the patient and relax into what the hospital had to offer in terms of therapy and structure.

You may wonder what it is like to be a patient on a psychiatric ward. First is the environment. Every 30 minutes (depending on how high risk you are) someone checks on you, and they may just look through your bedroom window or knock and stick their head in to say hello, or they might just open the door without knocking to check in! Bearing in mind that these checks are every half an hour, it makes washing, dressing, and going to the toilet a bit of a challenge!

The bedrooms are decorated in a minimalistic way and this is done so there is nothing that can be used to harm oneself or tie a ligature from. All belongings are searched on admission and thereafter when anything new is brought onto the ward.

Second is the routine of the ward. Smoking breaks prove to be a challenge and can be a cause of great distress for those that are formally detained, under section of the Mental Health Act 1983, as they are not allowed to leave the ward. Many a time there might be conflict between staff and nicotine-deprived patients wanting to go out for a smoke but are unable to due to their section! On the whole though, smoking breaks are given, but only one break per hour. This can be a good time to get to know others on the ward. Before you go out, you have to fill in a form describing your mood and it ascertains the risk you could be to yourself or others.

The communal area of the ward environment can be tricky to negotiate at times! There can be times when it is quiet and peaceful and you are able to watch television comfortably or have a chat with a member of staff or another patient in relative peace; however, there can be times when the communal area is extremely noisy and overwhelming. There may be the television on, a patient listening to music without earbuds, several conversations going on at once and another patient starting to get distressed or agitated and the ward becomes an unpleasant place to be. It was during those times that I would go back to my room, however if I was feeling anxious and overwhelmed, the staff would encourage me to sit out in the communal area so that they could monitor me and also for it to be a means of distraction. You don't want to be on your own with escalating thoughts as that is when you are tempted to cause injury to yourself.

Third, mealtimes can be difficult, sometimes because the food is not as appetising as it could be, but also because of negotiating where and who to sit with! Sometimes even standing in the queue can cause quarrels amongst the patients, as a schizophrenic person may think you are talking about them behind their back and retort in an unfriendly manner!

Fourth, during the week a patient is expected to formulate a routine and take part in the Occupational Therapy activities that take place on and off the ward. At first, I found these activities to be patronising, however as I progressed with my admissions, I found these sessions to be useful and a source of comfort and inspiration. Activities ranged from art, to Zumba, to mindfulness sessions, to going for a walk to a local café. To begin with, I hated these walks as I didn't want to be associated with 'those' people and was highly embarrassed about having a mental health illness. In time, as acceptance began to be imbedded, I didn't mind being seen with a random group of people out on a walk!

My favourite activity on the ward was a weekly session called Creative Expressions which was led by a freelance poet. I learnt that I could be creative in my writing and enjoyed writing poems. Here are two of my favourite poems that I wrote:

Opportunity

Opportunity comes with the passing of dreams,

Life so empty; or so it may seem,

Opportunity then comes with passion and flare,

Thoughts of sharing those dreams – do you dare?

Opportunity comes when silence is raw,

You look and look, is it truth or a flaw?

Opportunity comes in the silence of night,

Like owls flapping wings as they take their flight.

Opportunity comes with the sharing of day,

Words of wisdom, thought and play.

Opportunity comes with the sharing of speech,

The experiences of others, they too can teach.

Fairy Wings

Fly away fairy, where will I go?
I'd love to fly with the unicorns
in a rainbow of colours
Fly to Neverland
play with the Lost Boys
Grant them wishes
so their dreams come true.
One more visit with their loved ones
Where souls are resting
give them a heavenly blessing
Oh, to see my grandmother again
meet my brother David
who took up his angel wings
far too early in life.
Then fly away fairy, where next?
To sprinkle rainbow dust on clouds of silver
onto soft, wet, dewy grass…

Fifth, 'ward round' is the time of the week when you get to talk your treatment plan over with the consultant psychiatrist and can sometimes be a source of great stress. Patients sectioned under the mental health act might get anxious about how much leave they could be given off the ward, and whether there were grounds to have their section removed. I found ward round quite intimidating as there would often be up to ten people in the room, and sometimes some personal questions might have been asked, of which I would offer a guarded reply. I often found myself in tears during them, unable to speak, as the questions I had been asked cut like a knife into the heart of my being. The consultant did not mean to be unkind, he was just doing his job and exploring what was going on inside my head and understanding my way of thinking.

Here is another poem I wrote describing my emotions with regard to ward round.

Don't Look

Don't look inside my mind today, I'm scared of what even I might see,

Prisoner to where inner demons' prey,

No places to hide,

No place for thoughts to be.

Don't look inside my mind today,

I've cried some tears of pain,

I'm waiting to hear what the doctors say,

Some hope I wish for, to tell me I'm not insane.

Don't look inside my mind today,

It's grubby and untidy with dirt,

I try to not be as hard as clay,

But the way my thoughts are, I hurt.

Don't look inside my mind today,

Your look is too intense for me,

It's cold in here with no room to play,

I can't fathom the way I should be.

Don't look inside my mind today,
The focus of emotion is too much to bear.
I can't keep danger at bay,
I want to rock, and sit, and stare.

Don't look inside my mind today,
I feel angry at myself and hate the way I feel,
To shout and scream seems obvious; but is there another way?
I want to fall to the ground rather than stand or sit or kneel.

Don't look inside my mind today,
You prob and probe, but what's inside?
I don't want the thoughts there, but they seem to stay,
I want to foster a place where calmness and peace abide.

Lastly, getting used to the other patients could be a challenge. It is not always apparent why other people have been admitted, although some are quite open and will say why. There are some who have been admitted, like me, due to an overdose or an exacerbation of a personality disorder, others have unstable schizophrenia, some need stabilising on their medication or need a medication review. Some people are happy to talk to you and join in friendly conversation, whilst others keep to themselves, whilst others are so manic that they are uninhibited and will be noisy and not care what is going on in their surroundings. Some people spend the day laughing and talking to themselves, whilst others may spend the day in tears due to their depression. It is a mixed bag, so to speak, and takes some adjusting to feel your way around the ward and blend into the community.

Then it is important to get to know the staff and work out who you feel the most comfortable talking to. I am in awe of the staff as they work so hard to ensure that each person is getting the most out of their admissions. I worked with staff to formulate my Safety Plan, and this was helpful with becoming aware of what I needed to do to stay well, what was not so good for my health, what my triggers were for dipping in mood, and what was helpful for hospital staff to do or not do.

I often I wonder about The Perpetrator of my rape – I'd ask him: do you think you could be strong enough to work through all these issues? Have you ever been put in a place that invades your sense of privacy? Have you ever felt awkward with a group of people you don't know? Have you ever visited somewhere that feels alien to you, but you know you're going to have to stay there for a while? Prison comes to mind, Perpetrator. That's where you should go to experience all these strange emotions! But the difference would be that you are being punished for breaking the law, rather than being protected for your own health. Something to think about, maybe!

CHAPTER 4

Learn to Be Human Too

Humanity, Life!
Walk, talk, see, feel, smell, hear, taste.
I recognise you!

I could not recover from the trauma of rape and depression without the support of my family, friends, professionals and medication. Each has played a vital role in my recovery and their acceptance and non-judgemental attitude towards me has been key to my ability to start to like myself again and regain some self-confidence.

Opening up to family about my illness and how it has affected me has been one of the hardest things I have had to do. It has been easier talking to strangers about how I feel rather than talking to my family. This is because I have wanted to protect them from the way I feel, about the rape, and my self- harming, and BPD.

By nature, I prefer to have a few very special friends rather than a large network that don't know me as well. My friends have been amazing in supporting us as a family through my hospital stays and the depression. For example, my neighbour has older children, and she has, at times, acted like a second mum towards my eldest daughter. My daughter has been able to text my neighbour when she feels she needs to offload and doesn't feel able to do so to either myself or my husband.

One of my best friends was based in the same building that I used to work in. On one occasion when the depression was really bad, I pulled up in my car with tears streaming down my face. An aspect of my personality disorder is that I have intrusive thoughts. These thoughts are what the title suggests: intrusive. They are not wanted and not deliberately thought of, they literally come into my head and can be devastating in nature. On this occasion, I had had thoughts about hurting my client base in a particularly gruesome manner and I was in shreds about them and didn't know how I could go in-to work having had those thoughts, or how I could even tell anyone about them. Any 'normal' person would think I had gone insane! On that morning, my best friend pulled up behind my car and knocked on my window. She could see I was crying (I was going to try and pull myself together and go into work) and called me out and gave me a big hug. She just asked whether I was going to call in sick and I explained about the thoughts I had had driving into work. She was great and advised me to call my psychiatric team to arrange an appointment to see the doctor. Well, after calling in sick to my manager, I managed to get an appointment for my psychiatrist the same day.

After describing the thoughts I had had, she started me on antipsychotic medication. Since then, I have had other really intrusive thoughts, and so those doses have been increased twice more, and since the last dose increase my mind has been more settled and I have not had any further disturbing, intrusive thoughts. I ended up having a month off work as I needed to be cleared by occupational health and my psychiatrist that I was fit to work again, given the nature of those first intrusive thoughts. My best friend had been my saving grace that day as she took charge and looked after me without being judgemental or condemnatory.

My friendships are very important to me, and I am thankful for them. At times I have cancelled scheduled coffee meet-ups due to anxiety and not feeling that I could cope with talking, and my friends have understood and just said that they are available when I am ready to be sociable again.

Employers have been fantastic in supporting me with the depression, especially in the early days when I was doing my Health Visitor training. One person in particular, Jane, was remarkably supportive and put up with my somewhat bizarre texts early in the morning and last thing at night. My personality disorder meant that I connected with her on an intense level, and she was amazing at managing me and guiding me with difficult decisions I had to make. For example, when the safeguarding incident happened at my son's school, she supported me through how to manage my dealings with the school and encouraged me to stand up for what I believed to be right and proper during the following weeks and months, to ensure the safety of my son.

It was Jane that I first disclosed the rape to, following the safeguarding incident. I was in work one morning and we were making a cup of tea when I was able to say why I found the safeguarding incident so difficult. I was in tears and Jane sat with me whilst I recalled the events of that October night. She gave me the confidence to accept that it was rape and instilled in me the knowledge that it was not my fault and that any sex without consent from both parties is rape. The reality of this set in, and for the next couple of weeks I would spend the early mornings in tears trying to come to terms with what had happened to me as a teenager.

On another occasion, she accompanied me to hospital late one night. I had finished a counselling session, and this had left me in a very vulnerable mental and emotional state. I telephoned Jane as I didn't know what to do and I sat in a church graveyard in the middle of town sobbing my heart out. A few bystanders walked past me not knowing whether to stop or not, however I was able to muster a conversation with Jane and get myself to my place of work. She was waiting there ready with a cup of tea, and together with my main manager, they decided it was best I go to A&E as I was in such a dire mental state. Jane was amazing and sat with me the whole evening until I was ready to be admitted to the psychiatric unit.

In January 2017 when I was returning to work after my second admission to hospital, Jane supported me in sending an email to my colleagues which went like this:

Dear All,

Having just completed my second week back at work on full hours I would like to thank you all for your support in helping me settle back in.

I have spoken to Jane and think that it is appropriate to share with you all the journey I have been on, not for wanting sympathy, but so it gives you an understanding of where I'm at now.

In the last 16 months I've had two crisis psychiatric admissions to a local mental health facility, the latter being a 12 day stay in November. I have had tremendous support from the Trust, family and friends to get me to a place where I can work again! As we know all too well from our roles, mental illness can strike at any time and to anyone. It has, however, taken me a long time to accept my diagnosis of recurrent depression and try to overcome the stigma that it so prevalent amongst the general public.

I am accessing as much support as I can, and as part of my recovery and return to work I would like to ask for your continued support, understanding and acceptance. Depression affects people in many ways and for me the biggest factor is my concentration, memory recall, and very leaky eyes!!! Therefore, please do not take offence if I am quiet and don't interact much some days – I will be using a lot of energy to keep my thinking positive; and please don't take offence if I have to sit quietly for my record keeping – I have to work hard at my memory recall! If my eyes leak with tears it's ok – I'm not sad, it's my brain's way of helping me not be overwhelmed. In addition, with OH's and Jane and my managers' direction, I am carrying a universal (lighter, less need for special interventions) *case load as I regain emotional resilience. I look forward to carrying a full case load, however I'm being given the time and space to pace myself and get back into the swing of things.*

Thank you for your understanding and very happy to answer any questions.

Christina.

Jane ended the email by thanking me for my candour and thanking the staff for their continued support as I continued my road to recovery.

I enjoyed and valued this relationship and Jane demonstrated leadership skills to an extraordinary level. Once I left the Trust, Jane naturally became less available, and it was appropriate for me to relinquish the dependence I had upon her. There are other people in my life now that fill that hole, although I don't send out texts early in the morning or last thing at night anymore!

My main manager was also very supportive in helping me stay in post. I had regular meetings with the Occupational Health consultant and on several occasions, she mentioned that redeployment may have to be considered due to the stressors of my Health Visiting role. My manager was keen to keep me in post and we discussed ways in which this could be facilitated – carrying a more universal case load was one of these provisions. However, in April 2017, following the incident of the intrusive thoughts that included my client base, I had a meeting with her and I raised the prospect of my continued work, suggesting that perhaps it might be better for both me and the Trust for me to hand in my notice. My manager was in tears with me, and we agreed that this may be the best way for me to determine whether it was the job that was making me ill, or contributing to me being ill, or whether it was something else. In this way, through not being deployed, or going through the disciplinary motions (due to the amount of sick time I had already taken) I was able to leave my role with my nursing registration intact, and able to reapply for a Health Visiting post at a time when I was feeling fully well again.

Following my first admission to hospital, I found a counsellor who practised privately and who had over 20 sessions with me to begin with. During these sessions we covered a number of issues, and I was able to put the rape into some kind of context in respect of my naivety and need to explore my sexuality as part of being a teenager. A large part of the work used Cognitive Behavioural Therapy to help me work through some of the unhelpful beliefs I held about myself, namely that 'I must be good', 'I must get it right', and 'I cannot let anyone down'.

Another therapist I had was a clinical psychologist. We met on a weekly basis for several months and she used Compassion Focused Therapy to help me move my thinking from being negative and destructive to being compassionate and kind towards myself. She used a mixture of theory and practice to do this, and very much utilised the therapeutic relationship to demonstrate compassion and how I could integrate it into my daily living. At first, I had difficulty retraining my brain to think positive things about myself, however over time and by doing nice things, such as having a relaxing bath, doing soothing, meditative rhythm breathing, checking in with myself as to how my day/week was going, I soon found that I was able to be more compassionate towards myself. This eventually extended out towards memories of myself, and I was then more able to consider my traumatic memories with compassion. So, in turn, this meant that I could regard my 17-year-old self with compassion and non-judgement and be able to forgive myself for being raped. This forgiveness towards myself then turned to anger towards The Perpetrator. During previous counselling I had thought that I had forgiven him as I found it easier to be angry with myself than to be angry with someone else. However, once I was able to forgive myself, the anger towards him blew up and it was during a hospital admission that I caused the most harm to my arms in anger.

After an inpatient stay in January 2018, it was decided that it would be appropriate for me to have a key worker in the community. My first left within the first couple of months of having them, and I was then assigned to Claire, whom I was able to form a therapeutic relationship with from the first meeting. She very thorough and supportive, and intent on ensuring that all areas of my wellbeing were covered. For example, we did a piece of work together that explored my life from birth to present day to see if there were any traumas/areas of health that had been missed by previous practitioners. I had a full blood scan and ECG to ensure there was nothing physiological going on to cause the depression and personality disorder. Claire also used various questionnaires to ascertain my strengths, weaknesses, where I struggled with relationships, and so forth. It was from one of these questionnaires that it was confirmed that I had borderline personality disorder.

My meetings with Claire ranged from weekly to fortnightly, depending on need. She introduced me to chain analysis, which became a useful tool in seeing how I escalated in my thinking, with the aim to prevent a crisis from occurring. Chain analysis is a curve that appears when feelings and thoughts are plotted against time. The aim would be for me to sit on the bottom line, which is where order and calmness sit, with crisis being at the top of the curve. Claire used this tool to help bring me back to a state of calm when it was apparent that I was starting to climb the curve.

Sadly, Claire left the Trust in early 2019, and I was assigned another practitioner. This was someone who already knew me from the community, and she had previously worked on the psychiatric unit, so remembered me from bring an inpatient. Zoe really helped me come to terms with the BPD and continued with the therapeutic work that Claire had started. Zoe was an occupational therapist by profession, and she helped me with the practical issues that affected my day-to-day life, such as structuring my day and implementing a routine. The depression used to leave me feeling worthless and lethargic, and I could easily go through my day lying on the sofa, watching box sets. Zoe helped me see that I needed to do some things that were productive as well as self-care and relaxation during my day. This helped me a lot and although there were still days when I didn't feel like doing anything, I tried hard to do a bit of housework and go for a walk in the evening with my husband.

Another person who helped me through the depression was the ward psychiatrist. It was my opinion that he was like Marmite – you either love him or hate him. Fortunately, I established a trusting relationship with him and over the 13 or so times I was in hospital, he got to know me and the way I think. Although some of the ward rounds were stressful as he asked some quite probing questions, most of the time I came out of discussions with him feeling as though I had had my brain rewired and my thinking patterns reordered so that I could function more appropriately.

Medication is something that I still take on a daily basis but is not something I am comfortable doing, as I think I should be able to cope on my own. However, medication has been very productive and a key aid to my recovery. I take two types of medication – an antidepressant and an anti-psychotic. I started on the anti-psychotic after I had the intrusive thoughts of hurting my client base. After the first overdose I had my prescriptions changed from having them prescribed on a monthly basis to a weekly basis. This helped to take away the temptation to overdose, and my husband keeps any over-the-counter medication locked away in a safe box. My family know about this and understand that it is a way to "keep Mummy safe".

Finally, there is my dialectical behavioural therapy (DBT)[1] team, and DBT clinical psychologist Lucy. I shall tell you more about Lucy and DBT in the next chapter.

---

[1] Dialectical behavioural therapy is a talking therapy pioneered by Marsha Linehan, for people who experience very intense emotions.

CHAPTER 5

Demons

Heat! Do you feel it?
Demons lurking within me.
Stay away! Away!

As I said I would in my last chapter, I will now tell you about Lucy. Upon first meeting Lucy, I knew that it was important to establish a good relationship with her from the start. She is very warm and friendly, and so I had a heightened awareness that I should project warmth, openness and honesty back. The first session I had with

Lucy focused primarily on introducing me to DBT and to the client-therapist relationship. We discussed the things that could jeopardise the relationship and things that would benefit the relationship. I said that I would try and be as open as I could be, and we took this further by agreeing that Lucy could push me further if she felt that I was holding something back. We also agreed that it would be ok for me to say that if I could not talk about something further at the time, that Lucy would 'hold' it for me until a time came when I could talk about the issue without it causing too much distress.

We talked about how I was feeling at the time as I had had a couple of busy weeks and was feeling as though I was going downhill somewhat. We talked about my dark thoughts, established exactly what I mean by dark thoughts, i.e., thoughts of self-harm and suicide, and I was honest and said that I had started to have dark thoughts again, although I was trying to acknowledge they were there but then not give them too much attention. We explored my intentions on acting on those thoughts and I said that there was a supply of ibuprofen in the house that wasn't locked away and that I had thought of taking a considerable overdose of them. Lucy and I made a contract together that I would ask my husband to lock them away that evening when he got home from work and I was to text Lucy the next day to say I had done that. We explored whether this would be a difficult conversation for me to have with my husband and I said that he would feel sad that I was having these thoughts, and that I felt guilty about having them.

After this first session, I was admitted to a Crisis House as my thoughts had escalated in intensity. The second session primarily focused on my wish to escape from my head and to hibernate. Lucy said that this was a natural human emotion. She said that I had hit rock bottom because I was living for everyone else and not for myself. I agreed with that but struggled to see how I could live for myself when I didn't like myself very much. How could I learn to like myself? I loved my family, friends, home etc, but was that the same as liking yourself? I didn't know!

I spent a lot of the session in tears and annoyed with myself that I had showed my vulnerability so early in our relationship. Lucy said tears were ok and she was very warm and reassured me that how I felt was a normal reaction. We did some deep breathing exercises and sighing to conclude the session and Lucy asked me to use the practice of sighing to help with the dark thoughts. Instead of me wanting to escape from them, I was to imagine the dark thoughts leaving me as I breathed out.

The day after this second session I was transferred from the Crisis House to the psychiatric unit of my local hospital. This was admission number nine! Fortunately it was a short admission, with the main focus being to use the time to rest and refocus, and to restore a sense of routine to my day. During the stay I was challenged by an occupational therapist to write a poem and this is what I wrote:

The dark night of the soul – a lonely place to be,
The lights gone out, no hope for me to see,
"How are you, Christina?" people may say,
Do they see the empty pit I carry each day?

I put on my clothes with an ache in my heart,

An effort I suppose, but maybe a good start,

I paint a smile on my face to greet friends and acquaintances,

Nobody knows the thoughts that are my life's sentence.

But then,

A chink of light, so warm and so bright,

Seeps through the pain and gives some delight,

A dash of hope is caught with both hands and to treasure,

Maybe a saturation of joy can be one of great measure.

Our third appointment was slightly shorter as I had been discharged from hospital but was having suicidal thoughts and not feeling well. We discussed my thought processes and Lucy said that I could choose where to go with my thoughts and I could choose to avoid them. We went through where and when I got suicidal thoughts/thoughts of self-harm, and Lucy said that my memory links back to another time when I have been alone and had thoughts of overdosing. I was able to identify that it was usually late morning/early afternoon and in the kitchen that I had thoughts of overdosing and Lucy gave me this formula to read and digest:

A thought is an idea, or a suggestion, or an opinion,

It is actually a chemical reaction in my brain,

It is not a fact or the truth,

I can choose to pay attention to my thought or let it go or replace it with another thought,

It might not seem like it, but the choice is always mine.

This formula really worked for me and I have it written on a large piece of paper and stuck it to my fridge door. The idea of replacing thoughts was new to me, as is the choice of paying attention to my thoughts. I discussed the fact that thoughts link to emotions with Lucy and she said that this is true and that the cycle can then start all over again and that the choice is to interrupt that cycle of thought – emotion-thought.

The session ended slightly earlier than usual as my community support worker wanted to confer what would be the most helpful for me as I was having suicidal thoughts. We agreed that support from the urgent care and response team (Crisis Team) would be the most beneficial. This meant that someone would visit every day and support me with planning the day and help talk through any intrusive thoughts. They came to my home three times, and this was enough to help me through a difficult patch. I was discharged on the following Monday, with the provision that I was seeing the community psychiatrist on the Tuesday and Lucy again on the Wednesday.

The sessions continued in this sort of manner with a review of my diary cards (a daily log of my emotional vulnerabilities such as being over-critical and judgemental, and how I have used DBT skills to overcome them) and then a discussion about what has gone on in my week and we used critical analysis a lot to examine this. One particularly useful session was based on my thoughts I'd had when coming home from a stay in York and I felt unsafe being close to the trains at the station. We explored the thoughts behind my feeling unsafe and concluded that the trigger was seeing the police cars at the station and automatically making the connection between that and a time when I was in hospital and went AWOL and took myself to the train station nearby.

I had told a friend that I was planning on going to see my sister in York, and she informed the ward I had left without permission. I was feeling suicidal and was eventually found by the hospital staff who, together with the station police, escorted me off the platform to a place of safety. The chain analysis continued as I identified my emotion as fear and the reaction to fear is to run away, hence my perceived desire to jump in front of a train. Fortunately, when I went to visit my sister at a later date, I had the skills to act against the fear and I was able to get on the train safely and make my way back home.

I hit a brick wall in November 2020 when I had completed three modules of DBT and was starting to make real progress on my journey. I got to the point where I was so emotionally tired from learning new skills that I felt saturated and felt that I could no longer go on. I feared what else DBT might raise and what other demons were lurking in the closet. I expressed my tiredness to Lucy in a text one morning and she followed it up in the next session I had with her. I expressed my fear and that I feared being emotionally vulnerable, but she said that I was using my skills well and after doing some fact-checking we worked out that I was actually stronger than I thought and that although some of the emotions I was experiencing were painful, I was doing ok and coping. Before, if I felt a strong emotion, I would have gone into crisis mode, self-harmed and ended up in hospital. That was not the case now. I was able to experience strong thoughts and emotions, such as anger, and sit with them or work them through. I was close to giving DBT up and withdrawing as that would have been the easier thing to do, but with Lucy's coaching, I was able to see the benefits and realise that I could continue with the knowledge that I had skills and support behind me. I was lucky, extremely lucky, that I had such a strong support network behind me so that I could work through the humiliation and pain The Perpetrator had caused and hopefully come out the other side a much stronger, more confident lady. You see, rape takes away a person's sense of self. Rape invades the person's brain to the extent that you lose all confidence in yourself. Did The Perpetrator mean to do that to me? Did he mean to destroy the confidence I had as a woman? Did he mean to muck with my brain? I wonder, what was his childhood like? Was he happy? Was he raised as a confident child with lots of opportunities to shine? I was. I was given loads of opportunities to shine at whatever I set my mind to. I learnt to play the piano to Grade 7, I completed the Duke of Edinburgh Award Scheme to Gold level. I learnt to drive. I was given masses of love and opportunities to do my best and achieve. All this confidence left me when the depression kicked in. It has taken people like Lucy and DBT to rebuild me and restore the confidence I once had.

I was assigned a new DBT practitioner towards the latter end of 2021 due to staffing reshuffle. My new practitioner, Chloe, picked up where Lucy left off, and we established a therapeutic relationship quite quickly. As I

CHAPTER 6

Save Me

My eyes search for light,
Shattered words, shattered dreams, crash!
Save me from myself!

The DBT sessions were also guided by what I was learning in the taught group sessions. I enjoyed being part of the group. At first, being the newcomer was strange as everyone else knew each other and knew what to expect from the group. After a few weeks I began to settle in and enjoy the content of the sessions. There were challenges, for example some people didn't like to participate with their cameras on (it was a virtual group), some people talked/interrupted at inappropriate times, some people dipped in and out, and some didn't participate in group discussions. I found these challenges frustrating as it made the group disjointed at times and in the discussions I felt the pressure to lead as no-one else wanted to come forward with ideas. It felt awkward and uncomfortable when people were inappropriate with their contributions, but the leaders were sensitive and compassionate and gave people the space to talk in a supportive atmosphere.

Upon reflection, the behaviour of others influenced the way I communicated with them. The group did not in itself encourage friendships to develop, however over time links were made and friendships formed. I recognise now that this allying may have caused problems for those who didn't feel so comfortable in the group and opportunity could have been used to help group members interact with each other more effectively.

These DBT sessions are divided into four categories and are repeated to allow for the material to really take effect. The first module was Compassion, and although I had previously done compassion focused therapy with my psychologist, it was useful to return to the material and it was covered in more detail and in a different format. The first thing we did in the module was consider some the of the myths associated with being compassionate and I found this challenging. To be compassionate to yourself means you have to like yourself and I did not. Throughout the module I worked on being kind to myself and give myself permission to feel certain emotions and not run away from them. These emotions were shame and guilt, in particular. Lucy had already identified that I ran away from shame and extreme emotions, so this was something I really had to work on.

The second module was Emotional Regulation, and I found this module just as challenging. Again, we explored the myths around emotions, and I struggled with this as I had grown up believing that all negative emotions are bad. During the seven weeks or so, I learnt to recognise and acknowledge negative emotions such as anger, guilt, and shame, and sit with them without feeling that I was a bad person or that people would not like me because I was having a day where I was not always trying to be happy and cheerful. Anger was a particularly difficult emotion to sit with as I started to recognise that I could feel anger towards The Perpetrator of the rape and not feel guilty about it. This was very difficult for me and incurred some intense urges to want to self-harm as I had not previously had any way to express deep rooted anger. I learnt to vocalise that I felt angry, and this helped take away any secrecy of self-harming. My husband was supportive of this, but I was very aware of not letting the anger make me bitter.

I also started to recognise when my thoughts were potentially triggering and learnt how ruminating on thoughts was not beneficial to my methods of coping as the ruminations could quickly get out of control and lead to thoughts of self-harm and suicide. I learnt to capture the unhelpful thoughts and let them pass, as if on a cloud. This is not to say that I was dismissing the thoughts or avoiding them; I would simply let them come, acknowledge them as thoughts, but also let them pass and allow the disturbing thoughts to be replaced with more cheerful ones that I had more control over.

Anger. It's not a nice emotion and one that I found very hard to accept without feeling shame and guilt. It also meant that I could stop feeling angry with myself but start to feel angry towards others. I thought that I had started to forgive The Perpetrator, but actually I had been in denial and had buried my anger so deep that all it did was hurt myself. So now, I feel angry. I feel angry that he made me feel ashamed of my body. I feel angry that he took advantage of my innocence. I feel angry that he took my virginity. I feel angry that memories of what he did have prevented me from trusting others. But I also feel thankful, as without all this therapy I would not have learnt to truly experience the full range of human emotions. I feel like I am coming back to life.

The third module was Distress Tolerance, and this was a more skills-focused course whereby each week we would explore skills that could be used during times of extreme distress or crisis. It also explored skills that could be used for more chronic times of distress. I found the course to be helpful, but challenging, as we were expected to practise the skills even if we weren't in crisis. During the course I did have a two-week episode of feeling suicidal and did in fact take an overdose of medication. On this occasion I was not hospitalised and the mental health teams I encountered coached me to use my DBT skills. This was hard to begin with as I felt unsafe to be on my own and my husband had to be present at all times to help me feel safe and secure. In a one-to-one session with Lucy we explored what had triggered the crisis, and we identified that it was a piece of work that I'd been set to explore why I try to be perfect/try to achieve 100% in all I do. The particular area of my life that I had been exploring was my marriage and the unseen rules I had set myself for my marriage. Once Lucy helped me to acknowledge that I didn't have to live by those rules, I tore up the list I had written, and this gave me the freedom to live my life and with my husband without the pressure of unsaid rules. Of course, I have my marriage vows to live by, but apart from that my husband

and I can live our lives as we shape them and not by what other people's agendas or expectations/influences are.

Once I had the courage to do this exercise of tearing up the hidden rules, I started to explore other rules that I had set myself in other areas of my life, i.e., in friendships, parenting, etc. I started the journey of accepting that "I was enough" and stopped trying to attain perfection.

During this module, there was also a section of skills that explored the role of faith/religion/spirituality/God. Whilst I won't go into details in this chapter about my faith and relationship with God, it gave me the encouragement to pray and read spiritual verses. This would act as a skill and be beneficial to me. There was a book on our bookshelf that my husband had bought with 365 daily readings within it, and I picked up the book and started to read an encouragement each day. The first reading had a verse which said: 'I choose life'. This hit home as I had only just come out of my two-week crisis and overdose, and I felt like I was being given the choice to live or die/stagnate. I chose to live and in doing so, I felt another release of pressure in having to achieve perfection. The yearning of wanting to put my life on pause or to hibernate for six months (which is what I was hoping the overdose would achieve) was replaced with a deeper satisfaction and thankfulness for what I've got and to make the most of each day.

The fourth module was Interpersonal Relationships, and it was a module that I struggled to engage with as I thought that I was good at communicating. However, over time, the skills taught in Interpersonal Relationships served me well, especially when I needed to be assertive in expressing a wish or want. There is a model that is used which basically allows you to describe your needs, express how it makes you feel, and assert your desires in a polite fashion. I used this model for a particular ward round during a hospital admission as I wanted to get some answers for my care and how I was feeling.

CHAPTER 7

Man in the Mirror

Mirror, Image, See.
Reflect on how I can change.
Shine! Look within. Shine!

Another turning point for me was Christmas 2019. My husband saw an advert for a post with a local mental health charity and thought that the role looked suitable for me as it could be part-time, and it was looking for people sympathetic to those with mental health issues. Not taking the advert too seriously, I sent in my expression of interest over a glass of wine. Surprisingly, I was invited to apply more formally and this time I took the application seriously and progressed with it. Included within the application was a declaration of any mental health issues, so it enabled me to be honest and disclose my current mental health. A few weeks later I was invited to interview and was offered a post.

The first two weeks of the role were induction and proved to be challenging for me as we were doing self-harm and suicide awareness training. It triggered memories for me, however I was able to distance myself from those memories and put on a professional guise and this helped me through, along with several packets of cigarettes!

The other challenge for me was getting used to being up earlier in the morning and being in some sort of routine. I enjoyed getting ready for work and bought myself a new rucksack to hold my personal belongings, together with my work laptop and mobile phone. I had a lanyard with my identity on it and this meant a lot to me as it gave me a sense of belonging and feeling part of something important. A part of depression is that you lose a sense of self, so this really helped my self-esteem.

The team I worked with were great and friendly, and we soon developed a support network. The management team were also supportive and when I had a hospital admission in May 2020, they sent me a card and flowers and allowed me a couple of weeks off after I was discharged to get myself back on my feet. The admission that time was triggered by a DBT session in which sex had been mentioned when talking about states of arousal and this sent my head into turmoil. The other trigger was that someone at work had talked about people with mental health problems, particularly people who threaten suicide, as being “all the same”. This really upset me because of the dismissive tone that was used by my colleague, and I was shocked that they would classify people with mental health problems all in the same category. After my discharge I had several one-to-ones with my DBT coach and we discussed these triggers at some length.

I managed to remain in employment with the charity for four months, but then during one shift I overheard a nurse talking to a client about suicide over the phone and this struck too close to home for me to manage. I realised that perhaps I wasn't quite ready to be exposed to discussions like that and that the role was too personal for me to manage at the time. I had full support of my family and the management team and handed in my notice. I felt sad that I had had to give up work but was relieved that I had the insight into my own health and that what mattered was that I remain stable and well, for the benefit of myself and family.

Although the time in employment was short, it had given me great confidence in knowing that I was employable, even with a mental health condition, that I was able to work well within a team, and that I could hold down a job. The time following this allowed me to fully engage with being a homemaker and concentrate on getting fully well. I still had not gone six months without having a hospital admission in three years and so this was still a pivotal time mark for me. Time between hospital admissions and length of stay were my markers for how well I was managing with my mental health and how I was doing emotionally. It was during the immediate time after I finished with the charity that I decided to pursue writing this book, if only for myself rather than for others to read.

Shortly after leaving the mental health charity, we were offered the use of an allotment – I had applied for one the previous summer and forgotten all about it. I was aware that research suggested that gardening was good for mental health, but I couldn't really understand why. When we got involved with the plot, sowing seeds and plants, watering them and seeing them grow, I realised that it was quite therapeutic and good for the soul. I enjoyed being outside and being with nature and appreciating how things grow. The first vegetable we took home was a courgette and my husband and I enjoyed it sautéed in a little bit of butter!

In the summer of 2020, I also felt determined enough and had enough hope to tackle the six stone I had gradually piled on during the course of the depression, and started an NHS-based health regime of a calorie-controlled diet and daily exercise. I had tried to diet on various occasions but gave in easily as I had been a comfort eater and used food to satisfy me when I was bored, upset or angry. With my DBT skills gradually developing, I was able to challenge the thoughts of boredom and anger and channel the energy into something else, rather than seek food for solace. My relationship with food remains a challenge, as when I am admitted to hospital, I have the tendency to overeat, which is not helpful!

I found exercise more of a challenge, and although my GP had recommended that I exercise daily a few years previous, I hadn't taken her advice. Exercise is also known to be good for mental health and this is where the paradox lies. In order to be able to exercise, you need to be motivated to leave the house and have the energy to do some light exercise, even if its walking at a steady pace. Until the summer of 2020, I had not had this sort of energy or determination, but with the support of my husband I managed to start an exercise regime of walking, and occasionally went for a bike ride. I quickly started to feel the benefits of this exercise mentally and gradually started to look forward to my daily exercise. I also started taekwon-do and that gave me the opportunity to not only get fit, but the discipline and encouragement was a great booster and, when in class, enabled me to forget the worries of the day and be totally absorbed in what I was doing.

CHAPTER 8

This Woman's Work

Breathe; heartbeats dum-dum.
Giving life, giving strength, hope,
My tears run, no sound.

So, life was going smoothly for a while, and I hadn't had a hospital admission for two and a half years. In 2022 I was offered a post as a Peer Support Worker within the local Trust's crisis pathway. I was welcomed into the team, and I started to find my way in the newly appointed post and made connections with other peer support workers. Family life was going smoothly too, with our eldest daughter settled into university life and visiting home as and when she felt the need for some home comforts!

It was in November 2022, following one of these impromptu visits, that I had a dip in my mental health that rocked me to the core and shocked those who knew what was going on. My daughter had left to go back to university on the Thursday morning, and by Thursday lunchtime I was planning how I would overdose, but first poison my family with the rat poison that we had stored in the garage. I didn't want to kill them but couldn't bear the thought of being dead myself and not having my family with me. I called the local mental health support number as I was supposed to be going to work that afternoon, and it was soon escalated to the Crisis Team. I had an appointment with the doctor for a medication review booked for the Friday. My husband came with me, and a hospital admission was advised. I refused this admission and so the doctor advised that he would need a second opinion and that I would need to be detained under the Mental Health Act. The weekend passed in a blur and a doctor came to the house Monday lunchtime. By 6pm that Monday evening, I was back in psychiatric hospital. I felt so angry with this admission, as what I was thinking seemed to make total sense to me. I wanted to end my life and those of my husband and children. My mind had flipped through rational, logical, cold thoughts that made sense to me, which were totally devoid of any emotion and empathy.

I felt so guilty for the pain I had caused my family historically from my being mentally unwell, and for failing to be there for my teenage daughters when they needed me the most.

I was sectioned for 14 days, and the admission lasted six to seven weeks in total. The team of occupational therapists, nurses and psychiatrists all supported me in my recovery and encouraged me to explore other ways in which to engage, such as using my senses to help with self-soothing when distressed.

Life settled for a few weeks at home, and then in March I took another turn and had thoughts of harming my daughter. She had just bought herself a motorbike and my maternal, protective instincts kicked in and I had the awful urge to harm her, again it was in an effort to protect her from the awful things in this world. I felt so unsafe being around her that I went and sat in my car and contacted the mental health hub for support. As there was a delay in getting back to me with a solution to how I was feeling, I contacted the police. They were amazing and came quickly. My husband arrived home from work the same time as they arrived, and they supported me in being able to go back inside and be with my family. By this time the mental health hub had contacted me and arranged for me to see the community psychiatrist the next day. The next day my husband came with me to see the doctor and he recommended another hospital admission. There were no beds readily available, so he prescribed some different psychotropic medication, and I took that for around two weeks. By this time, I was feeling calmer and better and didn't end up needing the hospital admission in the end.

I remained on long-term sick leave, but sadly at the end of April 2023 I took another dip. It was whilst my family were out that I went looking for some lorazepam that I knew my husband had hidden from me, and I took an overdose with alcohol. I was admitted to hospital and stayed on the medical assessment unit for 10 days until a psychiatric bed became available.

This admission lasted for just over four weeks and in that time I came to understand and accept some revelations:

- I am allowed to be happy. One day my sister had had a long conversation with me, and she said, “Christina, you know you are allowed to be happy?” This really registered with me and I took to heart what she had said.

- I am enough. This was discussed with me during a session I had had with the link personality disorder practitioner on the ward. We had been talking about my expectations of myself and my own self-drive and self-esteem, and she said that I was enough. This again resonated with me, and I now have it set as a reminder on my mobile phone.

- How do I want to feel today? The hospital admission gave me space to feel a range of emotions and I enjoyed doing the craft activities that the occupational therapists did on the wards. I enjoyed how the activities made me feel and it was this feeling that I wanted to capture and remain with – the feeling of being calm, content and creative. I accept that it is not possible to feel like this all the time, but it is a feeling that I can aspire to when at home.

Another thing that resonated with me whilst in hospital is the saying: 'She remembered who she was and the game changed'[2]. I liked it so much and it means so much to me that I now have it tattooed on my right forearm with two beautiful sunflowers.

The sunflowers represent hope, and they look to the sun with the shadows falling behind them.

---

[2] Delia, L. (2019) Vibrate Higher Daily. Live Your Power. HarperCollins Publishers Ltd. London.

Life continued when I was discharged, and I was looking forward to the family holiday I had booked the year before. We went on holiday in August and had a fabulous time. It was on the way home that I had overwhelming thoughts of: what next? How am I going to manage the next year? My eldest daughter had her driving test in September and was returning to complete her third year at university; my middle daughter had a Taekwondo competition in Flanders in October, Taekwondo grading in November, and an application to the RAF to submit; and my youngest was returning to school in Year 11 and needed support for his GCSEs – it all felt so overwhelming! We arrived home and I went into overdrive, blitzing the kitchen! My husband could see that I wasn't right, but I was struggling to admit that I was dipping again. We returned home on the Thursday and by the Monday I admitted that I wasn't feeling well. I went to the local Crisis Café and the NHS worker referred me to the Urgent Care team. I saw them on the Tuesday and asked to speak to the consultant. He wasn't free until the Wednesday and after seeing him, I was placed on the list for hospital admission. This is what I wrote when I was admitted on the Thursday:

Can't believe I'm back here again – never say never again! I feel so empty and emotionally exhausted! I love my family and friends and it hurts so much. I just want to be no more. I don't want to cause my family pain, but I can't keep going on – I feel that they would be better off without me in the long run OR they need a well Christina that can cope with all that life brings.

I don't know what I want from this admission except answers as to why I'm in a cycle and keep dipping. I have urges to set myself on fire, or overdose or drink bleach or tie a ligature – that can't be good.

The admission was only two weeks long as I was able to de-escalate quite quickly and needed relatively little support this time. This was my 13th admission in eight years; however the consultant wasn't concerned. What he said was that it was the progress I was making in each admission that counted. My understanding of BPD was maturing, and I was starting to accept the disorder for what it was. The consultant said that I may have more admissions and I shouldn't be surprised if I have more. I accepted this and this permission to be accepting of being admitted to hospital took the pressure off me to have to stay well.

I met with my DBT practitioner on discharge, and I must admit that I wasn't feeling very well. I had strong emotions of sadness as I was feeling low about not being able to return to work and had just been awarded my disability benefits and was waiting to see if I would be awarded my pension early on the grounds of ill health. I didn't recognise the Christina before me. Ten or so years ago I was a very capable ICU nurse and then went on to complete my degree in public health. How had I become so unwell that the thought of caring for an intensive care patient who required Extracorporeal Membrane Oxygenation (ECMO)[3], haemofiltration (renal dialysis) and mechanical ventilation completely scrambled my brain?

---

[3] ECMO provides support to the heart and lungs to sustain life in a critically unwell person

CHAPTER 9

Bring me to Life

Where are you, my soul?
Come to me, back from the cold.
Home, where you belong.

Remaining on the ward as a voluntary patient was not all plain sailing! Once I had de-escalated from feeling so mentally wretched on admission to hospital, by day two or three I would inevitably feel desperately homesick and called home asking my husband to come and pick me up! There was one admission where I was placed out-of-county and that was horrible. I was an hour or so from home and although it was a private facility, the building was enclosed and lacked natural daylight, and the heating was on overdrive!!! I felt very hot and claustrophobic, and fortunately only stayed there for a week before I was recalled back to my local psychiatric hospital.

There have been several occasions where I felt the need to escape hospital, and on two occasions I actually did abscond!

The first time I decided to abscond was when I went to the train station and bought tickets to visit my sister in York, as discussed in Chapter 5. The second attempt was made on a different occasion, when I thought it was a good idea to try and walk home – home being 15 miles away and needing to cross dangerous junctions enroute. All I was thinking was that I wanted to get home. I was fed up with being in hospital and wanted to see my family. I didn't think about the risks of the journey nor the fact that I was mentally unwell and needed the care and support of the psychiatric ward. I thought that I was invincible and that nothing could harm me.

I felt liberated leaving the hospital and excited at the thought of going home. I was very frustrated when a kind, young couple stopped at a busy junction to ask if I needed help and they could see that I wasn't well. They ended up calling the police, the hospital, and my husband, and I was placed under section for 72 hours. I felt cross and disappointed with myself that I hadn't achieved my end goal. Although my husband was initially frustrated that I would behave in such a risky manner, he also showed me patience, kindness and tolerance as he understood that I was unwell. At the time I felt very vulnerable as I was not thinking coherently and scared of the capacity to which I could cause myself harm.

My thoughts at the time were of frustration as I was in such mental distress and just wanted to be free from the confines of the psychiatric ward. I felt that my freedom had been taken away from me and although I could understand that the ward was trying to keep me safe, I felt restricted and isolated because of the section. The section affected the way I communicated with staff. For the first time during my admission the staff felt like the enemy, and I was desperate to leave the ward. Although I wasn't hostile towards them, there felt like a real 'them' and 'us' barrier and I felt like I had lost all control. The power was with the staff, and that felt quite intimidating. My thoughts and feelings influenced my behaviour and communication with others, by making me wary and distrusting of them.

When I reflect on this now, I think that we can all do things with the best of intentions, but we still may pose a risk if we don't think things through properly. If I had expressed my feelings to a member of staff that I was feeling homesick, they may have implemented a safety plan to ensure that I did not try to self-discharge. I had completed a safety plan prior to going for a cigarette break (which is how I managed to leave the ward), however it was a generic assessment and I didn't consider my own personal needs at the time.

EPILOGUE

A devasting part of suffering with mental illness is the separation from community and feeling so isolated in your own thoughts and feelings. In the eight years I have suffered with depression, I experienced a huge sense of loss in terms of the communities I was once a part of. The biggest loss was that I withdrew from my spiritual community and felt a deep sense of shame as I did not think that the congregation I belonged to would understand my illness and the way in which it manifested.

As I have indicated, there have been many people that have supported me in overcoming isolation and loneliness – my community support worker, my DBT group, and my husband and family. There have been times where I have felt pressured to socialise or be with a group of friends, however I can now understand that my husband was trying to keep me in touch with others and feel part of a community. I thought that I would be bad company as my behaviour was so withdrawn and I didn't want to 'pollute' others with my illness. I felt guilty when my husband suggested that I do something, such as go for a walk, when I felt so lethargic and low. I couldn't understand at the time why he was encouraging me to do things when all I wanted to do was curl up and be insignificant. The depression was so real and debilitating that if I didn't have the support of my husband, I would have probably been successful in one of my overdose attempts.

It is painful to reflect on how isolated and lonely I felt in the depths of depression. The power of having a support network really kept me going and their determined persistence in including me in things was vital to my recovery. My family community have been a fortress and a stronghold. I have now come to terms with having BPD and depression and they are something I manage on a daily basis. I try not to plan too far into the future as I do not know what the future holds, but I remain in the day and try to remain steadfast in it. The most important thing for me to do is focus and care for my family and friends. Paulo Coelho, Brazilian lyricist and novelist, said this, and I believe it to be true: *Maybe the journey isn't so much about becoming anything. Maybe it's about un-becoming everything that isn't really you so you can become who you were meant to be in the first place.*